Dear Class

By Amy Husband

Published in 2014
by Albury Children's Books
Albury Court, Albury
OX9 2LP, United Kingdom
Illustrations © Amy Husband
Text © Rachel Elliot
The rights of Amy Husband and Rachel Elliot to be identified as the illustrator and author of this work have been asserted by them in accordance with the Copyright, Designs and Patents Act, 1988

A CIP catalogue record for this book is available from the British Library
10 9 8 7 6 5 4 3 2 1
Printed in China

Albury Books

For my sister, Nicki
A.H.

Dragon Class
Sunnybank Primary School

Dear Dragon Class,

This is the start of a very special week. On Friday, we break up for the summer. It's holiday time for our pet rabbit, Boris, too and one lucky person will get to take him home and look after him all summer.

Please write a letter telling me why you should be the one to take Boris home. I will then decide who will be best at caring for Boris.

When writing your letter, remember to:

1. Write your address at the top of your letter.
2. Start with the greeting "Dear" followed by the addressee's name.
3. Start a new paragraph for each new subject.
4. Close the letter with a suitable ending.

Remember, it's especially important to be on your best behavior this week. Good luck, everyone!

Yours sincerely,

C Brooks

Miss C. Brooks

The (Best) Table,
Dragon Class,
Sunnybank Primary School

Dear Michael,
I see you're writing
a letter. I bet you're
trying to get to take Boris
home this summer.
But you'll never win, because:
1. You're in trouble for breaking
your chair yesterday. 2. It's your fault
I laughed and got moved, so you're in double
~~truble~~ trouble. 3. Bruno would HATE Boris.
So you should give up and help me write my letter
instead, because I've got a much better chance
of winning.

Yours sincerely,

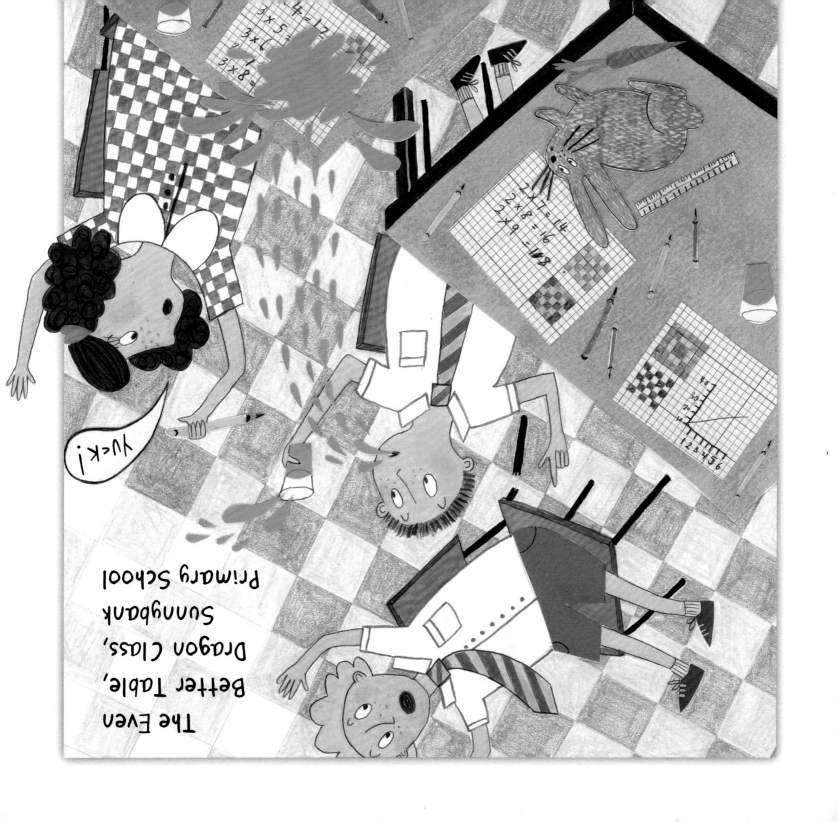

Dear Nicholas,

No, I won't help you write your letter. Write your own! It's your fault you got told off. I broke the chair by accident, you're the one who laughed and sprayed water all over Molly's math book.

Anyway, I'd be <u>LOADS</u> better than you at looking after Boris because:

1. Bruno would <u>LOVE</u> Boris and they could keep each other company.
2. I have loads of experience with animals.
3. I don't spit water everywhere when I laugh.

Yours insultedly,

Michael

My math book is still damp, actually, so pass your own letters. Molly

Just pass the letter! Michael

Boris would get triple-layered carrot cake with icing every day!

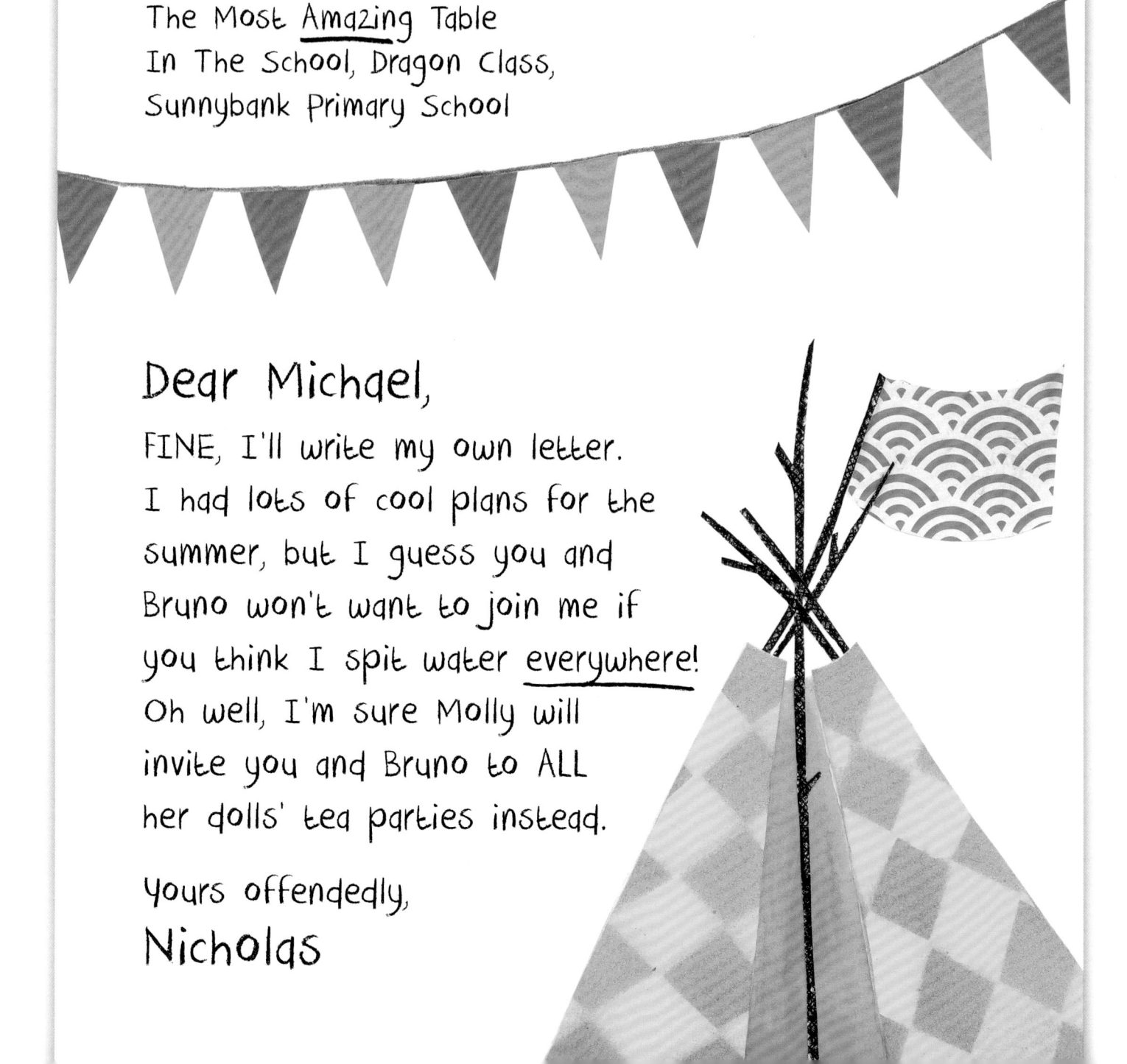

The Most <u>Amazing</u> Table
In The School, Dragon Class,
Sunnybank Primary School

Dear Michael,

FINE, I'll write my own letter.
I had lots of cool plans for the
summer, but I guess you and
Bruno won't want to join me if
you think I spit water <u>everywhere!</u>
Oh well, I'm sure Molly will
invite you and Bruno to ALL
her dolls' tea parties instead.

Yours offendedly,
Nicholas

I wouldn't invite either of you to anything.
Molly

Boris would get carrot pie and lettuce soup for lunch. →

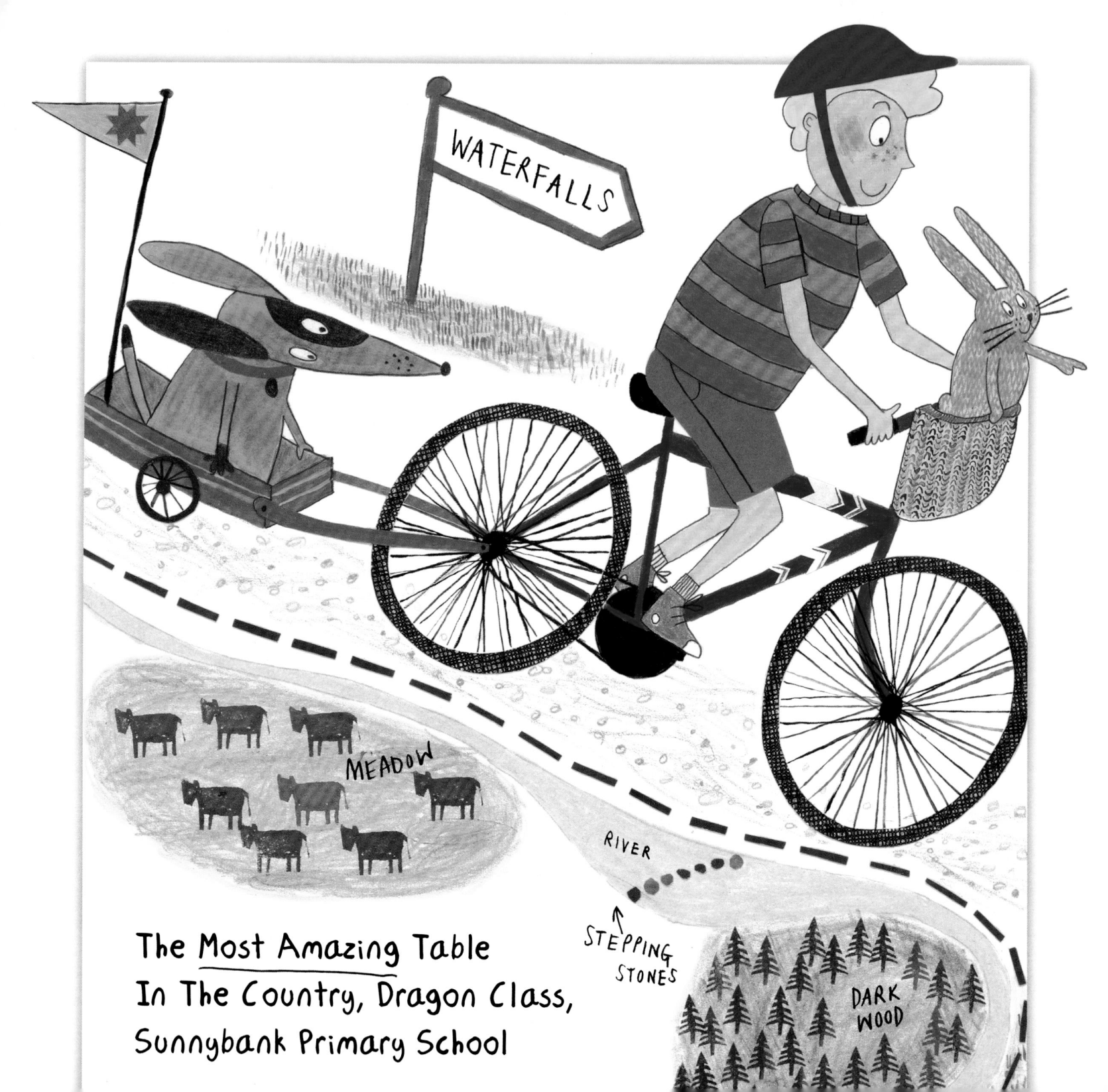

The Most Amazing Table
In The Country, Dragon Class,
Sunnybank Primary School

Dear Nicholas,

I don't like dolls' tea parties. And I had loads of great plans for ~~the~~ the holidays too. Me and Bruno were going to go on a massive bike ride up the river to the waterfalls with ~~Boris~~ Boris in a basket! I guess you won't want to join us if you're still cross with me?

Yours disappointedly,

Michael

What's wrong with dolls' tea parties?
Molly

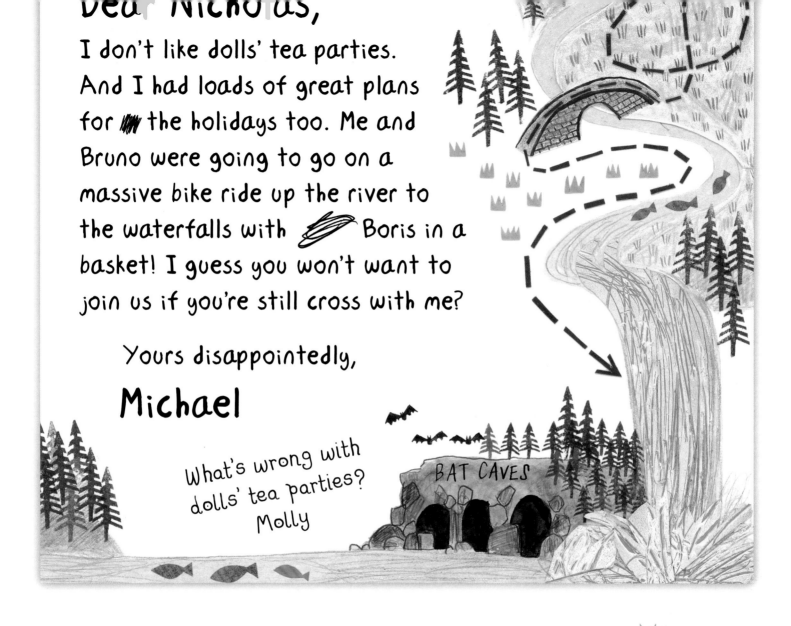

BAT CAVES

For breakfast, Boris would get scrambled carrots on toast with lettuce fries, grass ice cream and garlic slugs.

Dear Michael,

I don't like dolls' tea parties either. The bike ride sounds brilliant, but Boris and I had even better plans. We were going to have a Pets vs Humans soccer match in my garden. Do you want to come?

Yours hopefully,
Nicholas

Do I look like a postman? Molly

Yes. Nicholas

You are SO annoying. Molly

Just deliver the letter! Nicholas

What did your last slave die of? Molly

Answering back. Nicholas

For tea, Boris could have carrot scones with creamed ants and blackberry jam. ⟶

The Table That Would Be Even More Brilliant If My <u>Best Friend</u> Was On It, Dragon Class, Sunnybank Primary School

Dear Nicholas,

The Pets vs Humans soccer match in your garden sounds fantastic. Bruno would love it! And we could build the best, biggest-ever tree house in my garden.

Yours excitedly,

Michael

P.S. Does this mean we're friends again?
P.P.S. I'm sure Bruno will let Boris share his food.

For a snack, what about stewed cucumber with wormy custard and garlic slugs? ➔

The Table That Would Be
The Best If Me And My Best
Friend Were On It Together,
Dragon Class,
Sunnybank Primary School

Dear Michael,

Yes we are definitely friends
again. I really want to build the
best, biggest-ever tree house!
And how about going on a balloon ride?
Boris and Bruno could be the first ever rabbit and
dog duo to travel the globe in a hot air balloon!

Yours happily,
Nicholas

Dear Michael
and Nicholas,
I'm not passing any
more notes for anyone!
Yours sincerely,
Molly

Mmm - Grass chow
mein with spider rice
for dinner! ➜

The 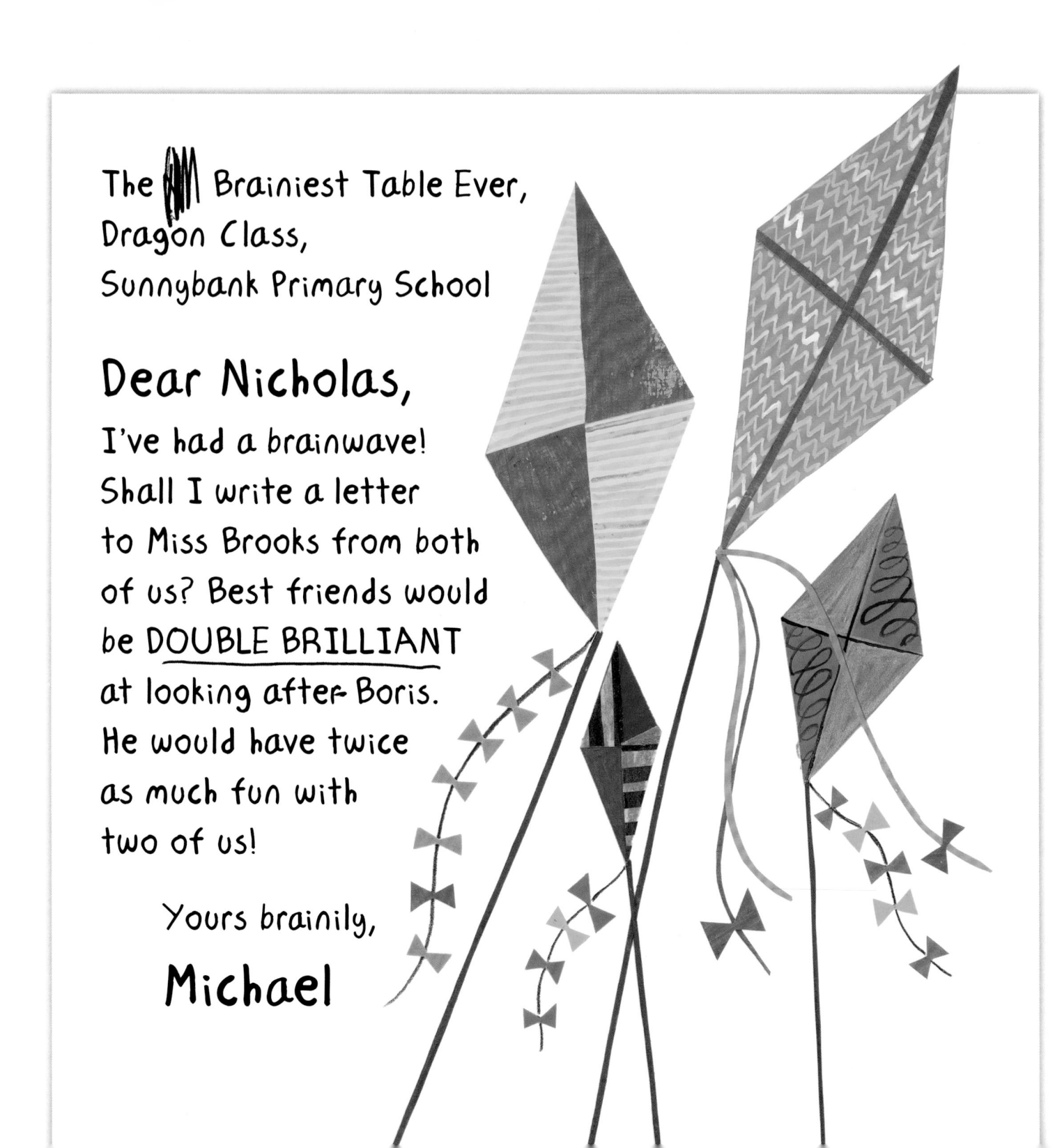 Brainiest Table Ever,
Dragon Class,
Sunnybank Primary School

Dear Nicholas,

I've had a brainwave!
Shall I write a letter
to Miss Brooks from both
of us? Best friends would
be DOUBLE BRILLIANT
at looking after Boris.
He would have twice
as much fun with
two of us!

Yours brainily,

Michael

Dear Michael,

Yes, definitely! Thanks for writing the letter, you're the best friend EVER.

Yours gratefully,

Nicholas

Nicholas and Michael – SEE ME.

Miss Brooks

Dragon Class
Sunnybank Primary School

Dear Michael and Nicholas,

Thank you for your letter. It was very interesting to read about the things you would do with Boris if you were allowed to take him home.

Despite your being naughty and writing letters during class, I was impressed that you addressed your letters correctly. Also, I think that looking after Boris would teach you:

- Responsibility
- Respect
- Nutrition

So I have decided that both of you will look after Boris over the holidays. I am sure that you will take good care of him.

Yours optimistically,

Miss C. Brooks

P.S. I notice you've been discussing what you would feed Boris –
maybe we should have a little chat about what rabbits eat.
I'm not sure they like wormy custard!

GO PETS!

A tasty treat for BORIS

- 1 cabbage leaf
- 1 dandelion leaf
- ½ carrot
- 1 handful of grass

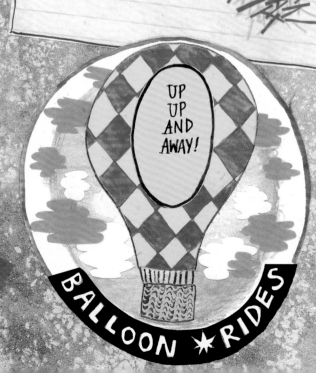

WINNERS

1

BALLOON ★ RIDES

UP UP AND AWAY!

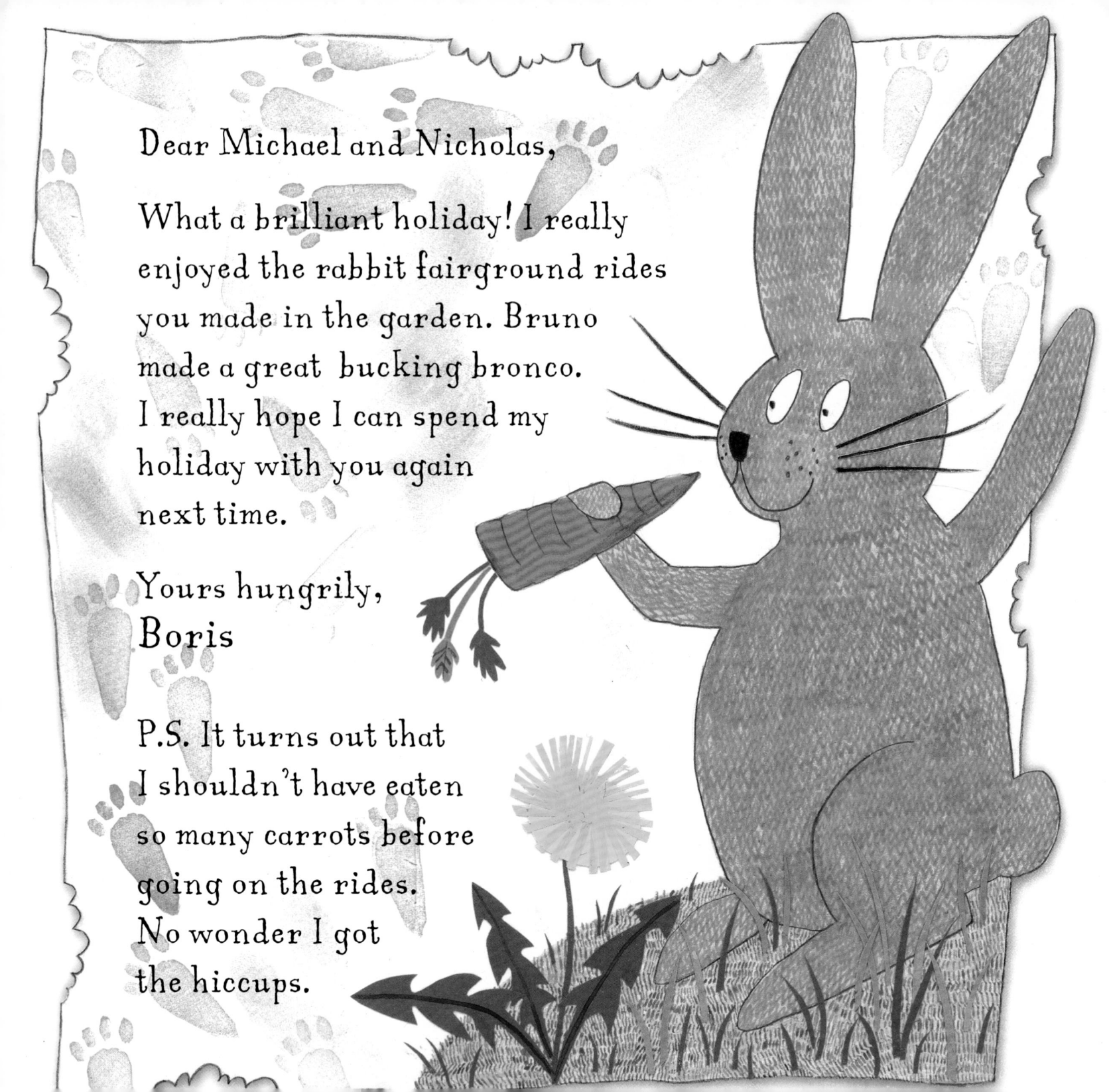

Dear Michael and Nicholas,

What a brilliant holiday! I really enjoyed the rabbit fairground rides you made in the garden. Bruno made a great bucking bronco. I really hope I can spend my holiday with you again next time.

Yours hungrily,
Boris

P.S. It turns out that I shouldn't have eaten so many carrots before going on the rides. No wonder I got the hiccups.